Campus Cutie

N. J. Salupo

Dedication~

For all of my amazing fan girls. I never could have gotten this far without you.
NJ.

CHAPTER 1

ORANGE USED TO BE MY FAVORITE COLOR. That was until I found myself behind bars, wearing an *orange jump suit*. Accused of the rape of campus cutie, Alexa May. Only I can't recall a damn thing that happened.

"Landon Crenshaw!" shouted a burly looking police officer. "You're free to go. Bail's been posted. Looks like you've got a guardian angel."

Katelyn Jacobsen trotted through the door, in a tight black dress and high-heeled shoes. Add the fact that her blonde hair was tied up into a bun and she looked almost lawyer-like. Her eyes searched the precinct for anything out of the ordinary. A corrupt cop, too many doughnuts, but mostly she was looking for me. What was she doing here?

A smile came across my face as her tall gorgeous frame moved toward me. She planted her hands on my shoulders, shook her head and planted a soft kiss on my lips. "Landon I was so worried about you. We're going to fix this. I know you couldn't possibly have done this. You're much too sweet."

The kiss felt inspired, her steady gaze made me eager to reciprocate, but *why* was she kissing me? I barely knew this woman. All I knew was that she was the best friend of the girl I supposedly raped. "Let's wrap it up kids," The officer snapped. "My shift is nearly over, so unless you want to spend the night in a padded cell, I suggest you get moving."

Twisting my arm, she looked over my shoulder and at the plump moron. He winked and smiled at her. "Pig!" She shouted. "Can we get him his things?"

A few minutes later and I'm following the sexy little beauty outside the doors of the precinct. She towered over me in those heels and once she turned to face my direction, I was just about eye level with her tits. Every guy's dream right?

Her car was right outside of the front steps, a 1987 cherry red corvette. The car was almost as beautiful as she was. The top was down on a warm summer day and I was already looking forward to seeing Katelyn let down her hair and watching it flow in the wind.

"Thank you," I said as she stepped into the car. "No biggie. You would have done the same for me, right baby?"

Baby? Why was she calling *me* baby? Nothing seemed to be adding up. All I could remember was going to some sort of sorority pledge party. I was excited to go because my crush, Alexa May was going to be there, and I never got invited to those types of parties. Now they say I raped her? Maybe I did. I didn't know what to think anymore.

I didn't know Katelyn very well at all. Until I got to college I hadn't seen her since the fourth grade, when we were assigned to work on a project about Italy together. Or should I say I did everything in my power to convince Ms. Redsen to pair me with her. You see, Katelyn was my first crush. This was long before there was an Alexa May. I had become obsessed with Katelyn, but I was just as much obsessed with science as I was with Katelyn.

By the time I was nine I had built a robot and trained it to offer breast exams to buxom hotties.

Worked to my advantage in the month of October with all those pink ribbons floating around. They just saw me as a cute kid with an overactive imagination. I saw myself as a smart kid that loved boobs. How could anyone not like Pamela Anderson in Baywatch? Any straight boy would have killed to be with her.

To say that I was shy would have been an understatement. The entire two weeks that I'd worked with Katelyn I'd barely said a word to her. One time she said, "Do you have any gum?" I said, "Sure." That was the extent of our conversation. I do remember how badly I wanted to kiss her though. I had dreamt about it nearly every night that year. It only took twelve years, twenty-two days, and forty-seven minutes before she planted those lips on mine and I have no idea why the hell she did. I was crushed when her family moved her to Florida two days after the conclusion of our social science project, never to be seen again, until now that is.

On her last day at Sunnyside Elementary I offered her my chocolate milk, only to be interrupted by Steve Miller, the freckle faced prick and school bully. "Gimme that," he said, swiping the milk carton from my hand and handing it to Katelyn. "For you doll." She gave him a wild-eyed smile and a kiss on the cheek. "Aww Steve. You're so sweet." Sweet my ass. The guy gave the word fucktard a whole new meaning.

I used to think back on how I should have tried to hold her hand. Kissed her. Every little boy wants his first kiss to be with his elementary school crush. I was in the passenger seat of her fancy ride and she had her hand on my thigh. Yet somehow, the only thing I could think about was Alexa May.

She cranked up the radio and started humming along to the tune as a Poison song came on the radio.

She must have still thought it was the 80's. Everyone loved Poison back then.

She slid her hand further up my thigh, near my crotch. I looked down at her hand with a puzzled expression, before brushing it away. "What's the matter baby? Don't you want to play?" No I don't fucking want to play." That's what I should have said. Instead I said, "I'm just tired. It's been a rough night." There was a time when I would have wanted to hold her and never let go, but now is not that time. Now the only thing I wanted from her were answers. Answers that I doubted she was going to provide me with.

I know that my project with Katelyn didn't work out back then but was that any reason not to tell me how I ended up in jail? I hadn't exactly asked her but I still felt that she should open her pie hole and spill the beans. Right fucking then. I sat next to her, trying to think of something to say to her that would convince her to talk. Nothing came to mind. I could see her smiling at me the way I once smiled at her. The only problem was that she no longer held my heart. That now belonged to the one and only, Alexa May.

That was the first time Katelyn had come to my rescue. But why?

CHAPTER 2

I LEFT THE BATHROOM IN A HURRY, turning the corner of Bowman hall and running towards my first class as a college student. I stumbled down a couple of steps in the classroom, nearly falling onto my ass and into the arms of the most beautiful woman I'd ever seen. It was the same sexy siren that I'd noticed months earlier at freshman orientation. All I knew was that her name was Alexa May and that she gave me a boner the size of the Eiffel Tower. I had been looking forward to bumping into her again, only this isn't exactly how I pictured it. I reached out my arm and it landed on one of the lecture hall desks. I clutched it trying to regain my balance.

"I'm so...so sorry," I exclaimed.

I sat down in a chair and looked at her face, unprepared for the type of beauty radiating from her skin. Quickly, I averted my eyes out of sheer embarrassment.

"I really should be more careful," I said."

"Yeah you should," said Alexa. I couldn't be sure, but I would bet that she was rolling her eyes at me. I searched my bag for a pencil as the professor began the lesson.

"Is there a problem Mr... *Crenshaw?* asked the African-American instructor standing before the class with an angry expression on her face."

"No-no problem."

"Then let's get started."

I continued to fumble through my bag when Alexa reached over and handed me a mechanical pencil to help me get started on my forensic science lesson.

I took the pencil from her hand and her finger tips grazed mine. In that moment I couldn't remember anything. Not who I was or where I was at. All I knew was that a gorgeous girl was sitting next to me, her skin brushing against mine. I knew right then and there that I wanted to hold her hand. That I wanted to kiss her.

"I should ask her out," I mumbled under my breath.

I dared myself to look into her eyes one more time, trying not to tremble. I did my best not to stare too much. I had never seen eyes as blue as hers. I'd seen actresses with eyes as blue as the ocean but none of them compared to Alexa May's. Looking into them, I wondered what it was about her that turned me on so much. I thought that maybe I could see inside her eyes and right into her mind. See what was going on inside of that incredible brain of hers.

Fuck! I'm staring. I just couldn't help it. I could feel a bulge forming in my pants as well and I set a binder on my lap to cover it up. I probably would have started stroking it right there if it weren't for the large crowd of people around me. I wanted her to like what she saw. I didn't want her to see me as that awkward misfit I was back in high school. I wanted her to see me as *dateable*. Stumbling and practically falling on top of her, probably didn't help my case. I wanted her to think I was sexy. Wanted her to have the same instant attraction as I did. No one ever made me feel that way. Not even Kelly Wong, the computer nerd I'd dated for approximately two months before she decided I was too boring, even for her. It was quite unsettling how people had treated me up to that point.

I wanted to be the type of guy that would take Alexa and bend her over the desk, right there in the classroom.

Alexa was just so distracting. Her hair was tied back into a ponytail and her glasses were held up by her button nose. She kept brushing a loose strand of hair from her face and it was just so...*so intimate.*

I pried my eyes off of her chest, where they had seemed to wander all on their own and began to take notes in a class that seemed intent on teaching me how to get away with murder. I tried to ignore the fact that she was in my vicinity.

My boner grew larger. I tried to ignore that too.

She was taking notes and her arm moved with every motion, giving me a bird's eye view of her voluptuous tits which were protruding through the top of her low cut sweater. Why did she have to have such nice tits? This couldn't be healthy for me. I dropped my eyes to my text book and focused on ballistics.

Because ballistics are interesting, and they don't have breasts the size of Texas.

Alexa leans over to write something down and the breasts I'm not thinking about lightly brush my forearm and cause my body to heat up like an inferno.

I casually jot down a few more notes and begin to sweat profusely. I'm suddenly drenched. Alexa goes back to fixing a loose strand of hair that has fallen out of place.

Ballistics.

I was thinking about ballistics.

But those goddamn tits couldn't seem to keep their distance and before I knew it, they brushed against me again. Except that time they grazed my shoulder and my body went wild like some love crazed teenager and knots formed in my stomach. Things were getting hot in that classroom. Too hot for my own good. My breaths got shallow and suddenly being in a forensic science class was the sexiest thing on Earth.

From the corner of my eye, I caught Alexa frowning at me, which could only mean one thing. The boob brush was unintentional.

That's too bad.

If I wasn't so shy, I probably would have tried to cop a feel. I could have responded with some witty, "you little slut" comment. Only the boob brush wasn't intentional and somehow that made it even sexier and my cock grew even larger. I was about to come in my pants. Why in HELL did she have to be so fucking hot?

She set down her pencil, her eyes still on the professor and stretched, pushing her breasts forward.

A sign that she was just as stressed out as myself. At least I'm not alone in my frustration. Though mine was more of a hot, distracting, zipper-brushing my boner frustration. Fuck pants. Shirts too.

Wait? Who said anything about clothes at all? I was NOT thinking about her naked. Damn you Alexa May.

I tossed my bag onto the ground and moved back in my chair, pretending to be fascinated by the lecture.

I fought back a groan. What was I thinking, living in the same dormitory as Alexa May? There was no way I was going to survive the semester.

Hell, I could barely survive that class and it was less than an hour long.

CHAPTER 3

I'D SURVIVED MY FIRST TWO WEEKS AT KENSTON STATE UNIVERSITY and it was time to let loose. Only that's not something I'd ever really done. It was a cool, windy October night following a thunderstorm. All across the campus you could see piles of colorful leaves, suggesting that autumn had arrived. Grey clouds still adorned the sky, indicating that the real storm was on its way.

I'd walked the half mile across campus to the Gamma Delta Zeta sorority house. A flyer advertising the party, still clenched firmly in my hand. It had been passed out to everyone in Biology class by a tall, lanky punk-rocker looking guy who had the words, "Save our souls" tatted along his right arm. He patted me on the shoulder and said, "Come check it out man. Plenty of available pussy will be attending." I read over the flyer that advertised the co-ed sorority pledge party and decided it might be fun. No one had ever invited me to a party before. College was going to be fun.

I entered the house that had Greek letters posted above the awnings, one of which was about to fall right off of the place. I could hear loud music blasting and was greeted by a guy who was wearing nothing but a tee shirt and covering his crotch with a cowboy hat. He handed me a beer. "Welcome to Gamma Delta Zeta buddy. Party on!"

I had to go to this party because I'd heard that my crush, Alexa May was going to be there. A little eavesdropping never hurt anyone. I'd convinced myself that it was time to start living. It was a new semester, a new school, and for the first time in my life I was open to adventure. After you graduate high school the possibilities seem endless. I was a lonely guy most of my life, having very few friends. Only one sort-of girlfriend. Now I was forty five minutes away from home and sadly that's as far away from my family as I'd ever been. I had however agreed to check in with them daily, which had proven to be a big mistake and caused me nothing but headaches.

The entire room was filled with strobe lights and the bass from the music caused the floorboards to shake. There were some couches pushed back against the walls and some scantily clad couples were making out on each of them. There were large beer kegs in the center of the room and hot girls were shot gunning Miller Lite from their taps, one of them was even topless. College was fucking awesome. Some other students were drinking out of red solo cups, leaning in close to each other to talk because the loud music made it hard for them to hear each other. Some of them nodding and laughing, others dancing to the beat.

A blonde girl wearing nothing but a t-shirt that said; *college guys---get 'em before they need Viagra* and a pair of thong panties caught my eye. She looked somewhat familiar. She had her mouth wrapped around the top of a Bacardi bottle and was heading for the kegger in the center of the room.

I couldn't believe it. It was Katelyn. She was a freshman at State too. The same girl I'd had a crush on as a young boy. I wasn't even sure that she'd ever known I was alive.

A drunk Katelyn handed me her Bacardi to hold, so that she could join the keg party. "Do I know you?"

"Landon Crenshaw. We went to…" She turned away and started chugging beer from a large tube that extended from one of the kegs. I tried not to get upset that she didn't remember my name.

She got up and wiped her mouth before taking her beer back from me. She leaned in close as if she were going to kiss me and said, "Do you have a big dick?" Her question caught me off guard. I didn't answer. "Well?" she asks again. "Umm…I don't know. It's average I guess." Katelyn put a finger on my chest and began to slide it down towards my crotch? "What's average?" I knew that my cheeks must have been bright red. No girl had ever acted this way towards me. Before I knew it she was cupping my balls and giving them a squeeze. "Maybe you could take care of me and my friend later." She then gave me a wink and let go of my nuts, returning to drinking.

That's when I saw her. Alexa May was standing in a corner and flipped her ponytail in my direction. She was the girl I'd come to college for. The woman I was destined to be with and again she was right there in the same room with me. God, she was beautiful.

I'd had a few beers by this point, which was a first for me. I was feeling great and decided I was done fantasizing about our non-existent relationship. I had a new found confidence and decided that I was going to go over and talk to her. I marched in her direction, squished my red plastic cup in my hand and disposed of it. Alexa looked just as out of place as I did, wearing her green sweater and an old pair of jeans.

"Hi. I'm Landon," I said. Just then Katelyn swooped in and put her arm around Alexa's shoulder. "I see you've met my number one biotch."

"This is Larry," said Katelyn.

"Umm…It's Landon actually."

"You two know each other?"

"We sit next to each other in forensic science class."

"Yeah he's the one I caught staring at my tits," said Alexa.

Katelyn lifts Alexa's sweater over her head, exposing a white tank top. She gives Alexa's tits a squeeze. "Sweetie…that's what they're there for. For people to look at."

CHAPTER 4

I WAS BLINDFOLDED and standing naked with my hands tied behind my back. Shivering on a cool fall day, I could hear a group of girls laughing at me. I was terrified as to what they were going to do to me. Why did they steal my clothes? Fucking bitches.

Soon I heard a couple of familiar voices. "C'mon Alexa."

"Katelyn I told you I don't want to do this."

"Alexa don't you want to be my sister?"

"Yes but…"

"No buts. Just do it. We aren't in high school anymore."

I could tell that Katelyn pushed Alexa in my direction as I could feel her presence and smell her plethora of body lotions.

I'd often imagined being naked in front of Alexa but being with her in front of an audience of drunken sorority sisters had never crossed my mind. I'd always thought it would be the two of us alone together in my dorm room bed, snuggled up until the morning sunrise.

"I'm Sister Annabelle. President of this sorority," said an outspoken senior.

"What's your name pledge?"

"I'm Alexa."

"And why are you pledging this sorority today?"

"Because my friend Katelyn wants me too."

"Not good enough. I'll ask again, "Why are you pledging this sorority today?"

"Because I want to be part of your sisterhood."

"Then are you prepared to do whatever it takes to become part of Gamma Delta Zeta?"

I could sense the hesitation in her voice. She may have even looked back at Katelyn for confirmation. "Y…Yes sister."

"Then kiss our brother that stands before you."

I'd hoped she wasn't referring to me but at the moment I seemed like the obvious choice. I had always wanted to kiss Alexa, just not like this.

She moved close to me, causing both nerves and pleasure to pulse through my body, something else rising to attention. Alexa reached out and placed her hand behind my head, pulling it forward until my mouth covered hers. This was exactly what I needed. A kiss from my crush. The woman I was instantly attracted to from the moment I'd first set eyes on her. This might not be how I planned it but it was definitely different, almost reckless. For the first time in my life I felt like I was doing something wrong and damn what a good feeling it was.

I slid my tongue between Alexa's lips and began to taste every dark corner of her mouth. Never mind that I had never French kissed anyone before. This was my chance. It was risky and erotic, and I was a part of it. This was a feeling I'd waited for my entire life. She continued to kiss me back, making me crave more of her. I needed more. I wanted to touch her hair. Imagined how soft it would be. I wanted to cup her breasts, but the restraints prevented me from doing so.

"I didn't mean kiss him on the mouth. Kiss him down there," said sister Annabelle.

I assumed she was pointing to my cock.

"On your knees pledge."

I moved towards her and kissed her again before she fell to her knees. I wanted to hold her. To take care of her forever.

I couldn't keep an anxious sigh from escaping my mouth.

"You're beautiful Alexa," I whispered as her hand reached between my thighs. I could feel her long fingernails tracing my skin. She was driving me absolutely crazy.

"Suck his dick! Suck his dick!" chanted a bunch of overzealous sorority sisters.

Once she wrapped her long fingers around my cock I lost all control and let out a groan. I began mumbling some words that probably didn't make any sense to anyone, including myself. I knew this was a stupid hazing ritual, but I didn't ever want it to end. She began pumping her wrist up back and forth and pushed my leg back with her other hand, which would have given me a full view of her beauty had I not been blindfolded.

I'm assuming, Annabelle grabbed Alexa May's free hand and placed it on my bottom, while her other hand now cupped my arousal. Soon I could feel her tongue against the tip of my shaft and the warmth of her breath between my thighs. She took me deeper into her mouth causing my body temperature to go through the roof. The risqué nature of what we were doing set me over the edge and my world intensified into a million little earthquakes, the same way it had the moment I'd met Alexa.

"How does it taste?" said Annabelle."

Alexa doesn't respond and keeps doing her thing.

"Oh yeah, she really wants this bad," said another member of Gamma Delta Zeta.

"She's good at that. Show our brother how it's done, said Annabelle. I could feel that her presence was within inches of me.

Again they started chanting, "Suck that dick! Suck that dick!"

"Take off that top sweetie." I assumed that Annabelle removed her top. "Get it wet. Deep throat that shit."

"Deep throat! Deep throat! Deep throat!" they shouted.

"C'mon rush. You want to be in the sorority don't you? You want to be a sister? C'mon girl show us what you've got. C'mon girl you know you've sucked dick before. How bad do you want to be in this sisterhood? Our brother really likes it. Stop teasing woman. Suck that shit baby. Give those balls some attention too."

I could hardly take much more. I was picturing her firm, round breasts in my face and her lips felt so good wrapped around my shaft. Within seconds I came, Alexa swallowing every drop of my warm spunk.

"Yeeeaaaaahhhhh!!!" chanted the sorority sisters, some of them clapping.

"Welcome to Gamma Delta Zeta sister Alexa," said Annabelle.

Then the girls took the blindfold and cuffs off of me and tossed a topless Alexa a purple shirt with Greek letters on it. I was still in the center of the room and everyone was staring at me as I covered my privates with my hand as if they hadn't already witnessed what I could do with it.

"Get lost nerd. We're done with you."

CHAPTER 5

I'D TAKEN A PART-TIME JOB, at the campus bookstore to make a little extra cash. It was my first week there when SHE walked in. She reached out her arm to make sure the door didn't smack her in the behind. She smiled at me or at least in my direction, like the nice girl that I thought she was. She'd been biting her nails that had been painted red and almost seemed embarrassed to be in the store. She was wearing a pink V-Neck sweater and I could see part of a black bra poking through the top. Her hair was still wet from a recent shower and she smelled like a mixture of kiwi and watermelon. That's when I said my first intentional word to her-hello-when most of the other employees would have just ignored her in her loose blue jeans. Where did you come from Alexa May?

She was dainty and pristine, my own little brunette version of Reese Witherspoon circa the movie Cruel Intentions, when she was still a virgin and hadn't yet been corrupted by bad boy Sebastian. She'd come into my store on a Monday, 10:23 a.m. Every day I rode my bicycle to this shop on the east side of campus from Burlington Way, the street my dorm was on. Every day of my life I'd been looking for someone like her. I couldn't believe that anyone as beautiful as her had been born into the same world as myself. I was trembling and in desperate need of something to calm me down. Too bad I'd left all of my anxiety medication back in my room. I watched as she turned her head left and then to the right, her ponytail whipping back and forth as she moved. She power walked through the stacks of books on her right, biographies, no, self-help, no (thank fucking God) and finally slowed down when she got to fiction.

My kind of girl.

She disappeared into the stacks and stopped at A-D. I could think of something else that often ran A through D. I may have been an intellectual, but my mind was in the gutter at least ninety percent of the time. Alexa wasn't the type of slut that usually came into that place, searching for Cliff's notes so that she could still pass after an overnight drinking binge. She seemed like a Jane Austen kind of girl. She was much too prissy looking for Stephen King, too opinionated to deal with the antics of Hemingway and too educated for anything printed later than 1980. I thought about going over and giving her some assistance but instead all I could think about was how loud she'd sound when she climaxed.

I wondered what she was going to buy. I could picture her as a little nympho beneath all those clothes. I wanted to be the kind of guy who flirted instead of the bitch that hid behind his computer, using Facebook as his only communication between himself and the opposite sex. I still couldn't believe I was staring in the direction of the same girl that had gotten me off over weekend. I guess we weren't going to talk about it.

Calm down, Landon. I knew that girls hated it when you came on too strong. I just wanted her to notice me. I wanted to go on over and ask if she had read anything from Salinger, my personal hero. That guy knew how to tell it like it was. I absolutely loved

Catcher in the Rye. My staring was interrupted by a young guy with a basket full of books. I went to ring him up. He handed me a copy of Shakespeare's Macbeth, which was only a front for the Sports Illustrated swimsuit edition at the bottom of the basket. People were often afraid to be themselves in public, myself included.

I packaged the magazine first as if it were gay porn and told him he should fill out the survey on the back of his receipt for to get a ten percent off coupon. He nodded his head, thanked me and was on his way. Alexa was still in the A-D section. I could see her out of the corner of my eye. As she reached up to one of the higher shelves, her pink sweater rode up, exposing a butterfly belly button ring. Alexa, you little slut. She grabs a book, Wuthering Heights and sits down in the aisle. I fucking knew it. It was Emily Bronte, not Jane Austen but close enough.

I wondered if she'd stay there all night until I closed the building. While I thought that some of Jane Austen's work was alright, the B section housed Emily Bronte's Wuthering Heights and just may have been the most boring book every written, with Grapes of Wrath a close second. Maybe I could go over and find her between the stacks after I shut the lights off. I could say something witty like "Excuse me miss, we're closed. What time do your legs open?" Maybe she'd look up and smile at me and say, "Right about now. They're always open for you Landon."

That jackass customer with the magazine was still in the store. "Hey," he shouts, interrupting my voyeurism. "Can I get my ten percent off now?"

"It's for your next purchase, Sir," I said.

"But I filled out the survey."

"You'll have to hang on to your receipt until next time."

I could hear him mumble some sort of profanity in my direction before exiting the shop for good.

People like that guy signified everything that was wrong with society. If he was that upset over a coupon, he might as well have just killed himself.

Just because I worked in a bookstore didn't mean I wasn't too damn gifted to work in one. I just happened to love reading. The man could have said anything to me and he would still be the same loser who was going home and jerking off to a bunch of fake looking models while I was there checking out a natural beauty.

Fuck You. You fucking prick.

I could hear Alexa laughing, as if there was actually one funny line in that entire shitty book. I'm glad it was slow at that time of day, just Alexa and I. I had her all to myself.

I finally built up the courage to go and talk to her. I wanted to know more about her, who her favorite rock band was, what color panties she was wearing. All critical foundations for starting a relationship.

Just from a couple of classes with her, I could tell that she and I were similar. People with type A personalities often were. Always striving to be the best. Second place just wouldn't be good enough for people like us. Our type always wanting to lose ten pounds, or learn a new language or know the greatest amount of useless information known to man. We were typically neat, tidy and organized. What we really wanted to do was get trashed with a good looking member of the opposite sex, take mushrooms and watch porn. Maybe even rob a couple of banks with the single push of a button.

She was giggling again as I approached her and looked over her shoulder in my direction before burying her face back into Emily Bronte. I could hear a text message go off on her phone. Clearly an iPhone.

Funny, I had pegged her as more of a Droid kind of girl. She checked her phone briefly before putting it back into her pocket and I give her a tap on the shoulder.

"So why do they call him Mr. Lockwood anyways? Seems kind of perverted to me."

I couldn't believe I'd just said *that,* and she actually listened. Such a doll.

She didn't have to pay attention to me, or make eye contact with the guy at the store who was picturing her in nothing but a pair of stockings and six inch silver heels, hoping she'd beg to be spanked later.

She never responded to my first statement, so I changed my tune. "You really are beautiful, you know that?" Her eyes lit up at my compliment, almost is if no one had ever told her that she was absofuckinglutely gorgeous.

I noticed that her hands weren't adorned with any type of frosting, no wedding bands, promise rings or purity rings for that matter. No sign of a boyfriend lurking around campus either. Looked like I had a shot.

I was pacing back and forth in the aisle behind her and flattered that's she was one of the few who read. I don't just mean the smut that girls read on their kindle device's so that the world doesn't know they are deviants. I mean the actual kind of books that you could hold in your hand and enjoy the smell.

I bet she came from a big family, at least four brothers. I could tell by the man hating look she often had on her face during forensics class. Either that or some horrible ex-boyfriends. Who hurt you Alexa May?

I loved that reading seemed to be her passion instead of movies or video games, or anything else that your typical mean girl might be into. I was hovering behind her and surprised that she hadn't yet told me to fuck off. I had gotten to see Alexa that day because the rest of the nerds were either at the comic book store or in a laboratory somewhere.

When she'd taken out her phone, I noticed that the pink plastic case was cracked, indicating that material things weren't all that important to her. I do have to admit to being worried that she was getting a text from her big-dicked booty call. In reality it was probably just her mother checking in.

After reading nearly the entire book, she got up off the floor.

"I think I'm all set."

I guided her to the front counter and began to ring up her purchase. She set the book in front of me and I noticed that her nipples were poking through her shirt. You want me bad Alexa. You just don't know it yet. She bent down, giving me an even better view of the melons and reached for a pack of Wrigley's spearmint chewing gum.

All I could think about was kissing her but instead I was standing behind a cash register, wearing a name tag and an apron. Hardly a turn on. She paid for her merchandise and I noticed that she was holding a purple flyer in her hand, advertising a frat party. Damn.

These types of flyers were becoming a common occurrence on this campus. I'd just have to crash that one too. See you soon Alexa May.

CHAPTER 6

"**ALEXA!**" shouted the coach.

I could see her from my front row seat in the bleachers. I wasn't normally one to attend sporting events, but when I'd heard Alexa was part of the team I was sure to get myself a ticket.

A pissed off Alexa seemed to ignore her coach and took a step in my direction. Her ponytail whipped behind her head. I wondered what she would look like if she took her hair down. It had been in ponytail form every time I'd seen her. "What are you doing here? Are you following me?" She had every right to assume seeing me around campus so much the last several days. "I'm here to watch the game."

"Sure you are."

I brushed my long blonde hair out of my face, sure that her response was full of sarcasm. The coach walked over to Alexa and put his arm around her shoulder. "Get it together. We've got a match to win," he said.

"We can't win. We're down twelve points," said Alexa.

"What kind of an attitude is that? Since when are you negative? You're supposed to be the team captain."

That guy was pissed.

I watched their entire disagreement and saw Alexa lower her head in shame. Still I couldn't take my eyes off her.

She looked so sexy in her volleyball uniform, a form-fitting green shirt with green spandex pants. The toned muscles of her long legs leaving me speechless. I wondered if she was there on an athletic scholarship. I had arrived slightly late to the game and now I was about to see if she could really play. I assumed team captain must mean she was good at this sport. I watched as she ran back onto the court, her chest held steady by a sports bra, but the perfect curvature of her ass made up for that. Damn girl.

Alexa shook her head and ran back onto the court. "Let's win this thing," said Coach Cameron, patting her on the behind.

Her head popped up and she looked like she wanted to kill someone. There were no tears in her eyes as she stared down her coach. "Give me the ball!" she shouted, ready to serve. I didn't want to be her at the moment. I'd had my share of put downs from my peers, parents, teachers and anyone else who'd wanted to take a stab at me. I was just glad there was no one here to chew my ass out right now.

Katelyn strutted into the gym and took a seat right next to me, her long blonde hair held in place with an entire can of hair spray. "Are you enjoying watching her, your little pecker growing as she runs around in those tight little shorts."

Sure it was fun to see little miss reserved running around the gym, getting all sweaty but I wasn't going to give Katelyn the satisfaction of admitting it.

"It's okay I guess."

"I bet you want to get inside those shorts, don't you," she said, sliding her hand up and down the inside of her thigh. I know how much you enjoyed that little hazing incident, having her soft lips wrapped around your…"

"Stop that," I said, sliding down the bleachers and away from her.

"Ladies!" Coach shouted as the old man paced in front of the bench. "We've got to win this one! Alexa get us started!"

Alexa served it up and the ball went back and forth until another beanpole spiked it over the net, getting our Hornets a point. Alexa looked over her shoulder and I burned my eyes into hers. I hoped she wasn't mad at me. It wasn't my fault that she was so goddam beautiful. I just happened to like looking at pretty girls.

A male voice echoed, "What's up sexy girl," and I shifted my eyes in his direction. Jackson Waters, the Harley riding, muscle bound, spiky haired, leather jacket wearing douchebag with too many tattoos had slid down towards Katelyn. All the girls loved this guy. I didn't really know him, but judging by the look of him, I assumed he could be described not only as a douchebag but a jackass, prick, asshat or any other word that came to mind. My eyes then darted back to Alexa who had gone over to the bench to get a drink of water and wipe her forehead with a towel.

"Stop drooling, Landon." Oh my God, she knew my name. Alexa May knew my name. She was only a few feet from me, and I took in her scent. How could she still smell so delicious covered in sweat. She still smelled feminine, scented with some sort of cherry blossom body lotion as her lean body towered over me. What a turn on.

She raised her eyebrows as I looked up at her. She was so beautiful, so perfect. "I was just concerned about you. I wouldn't want you to get hurt out there. Maybe you should pay attention to the game, instead of me," I chided. She stood muted for the moment.

"What's the matter, you interested in this rocking hot bod?"

I couldn't believe the things that had just come out of my mouth. That's when I looked around and realized that everyone was watching us. What had I done? I couldn't breathe.

I continued to stare her down as she ran full-speed back onto the court. "Bitch," I mumbled under my breath. She turned back towards me, without trying to give her old coach a heart attack. "Did you say something?"

"No. Not me," I said. I couldn't believe I'd called her a bitch. She deserved to be treated only with utmost kindness and affection. Taken care of like the princess that she was.

After watching for a bit, there was no doubt just how much skill Alexa had when it came to volleyball. I couldn't believe that her coach had been so rude to her. I supposed that was his shitty way of motivating her. He was doing something right though. Alexa May was one hell of a competitor. The Hornets had come all the way back to tie the game because of her.

She tossed the ball in the air, serving for the win. It went high up into the rafters. The players on the other team watched for gravity to bring it back down. The best player for the Youngstown Spiders, eventually hitting it back over the net. We were going to lose. That was until Alexa ran full-speed up to the net and spiked it right down their throats. The crowd in an uproar at the Hornets big win.

CHAPTER 7

I WAS NINETEEN YEARS OLD, in need of a haircut and too damn short but those were the least of my problems. I'd woken up naked in a bed next to Alexa May with no memory of how I ended up this way. I could tell you that it was October but not much else. I tried to close my eyes and remember how I ended up in the same bed with my dream girl, but nothing seemed to click. I looked around and saw a box of Chinese food, a pile of our clothes on the floor near the bottom of the bed and that goddam Wuthering Heights book on the night table. I'd hoped I'd fucked her. Hard.

I'd tried for weeks to have sex with Alexa, with no luck at all. She just didn't seem interested. Which I'll admit hurt my feelings a bit. What wasn't to like about me? I was a forensic science major, sure to make Dean's list and a mathlete champion three years running. I'm sure she didn't even feel one tiny ounce of guilt by making me feel like shit.

I'd been trying to get her to at least go on a date with me. She said no to that too. I'd been watching her meticulously since the day I'd met her. I watched her in the hot tub at the neighbor's pool party, in her sexy little pink bikini. I'd been peeking over the fence, fully intent on banging her someday.

I'd climbed over the fence, careful not be seen and hid in some nearby bushes. I'd seen her and Katelyn flirting with that Jackson guy. He even wore that leather jacket to a pool party. Clearly he had issues. I'm still not sure why any of them were at my next door neighbor's house over the summer. This was the day of freshman orientation and the very same day I'd met Alexa May. Well not so much as met but set eyes on.

Wow. What a View! She was gorgeous. I could tell that Jackson wanted her. Bad. Katelyn too. I continued to focus on Alexa as Jackson grabbed her wrist and pulled her straight into the hot tub, her glasses falling off into the water. Her head went under and she fluttered her arms until she reached the surface. "Fuck you," she shouted. For such a beautiful young lady, she sure had a potty mouth. Jackson followed her in and had his hands all over her, her back, her legs, her breasts. I should have been pissed off. Should have ran over and attempted to kick his ass but the truth was that I'd ran from the slightest hint of a fight throughout my entire life. Rumor had it there was this college guy that got girls into the hot tub and had his way with them. I'd assumed Jackson was that guy by the looks of things. He was going to pound her for sure and I was going to stay right there in those bushes, wishing those were my hands on her breasts.

She tried to fight him off, splashing around in the water. Most of the slutty little Vixens in my area, Lyndall, Ohio, would have just let him have his way with them. Not Alexa. She was just too damn feisty. If I'd learned anything in my short time on this Earth it's that everyone pays for pussy in one way or another. So, why should this guy get it for free? Guys fully expect to be taken care of after taking her out to a fancy dinner or buying her that Gucci bag. Even then some women still said no, which is probably why they got slapped around so much. She finally escaped his grasp and climbed on to the pool deck in search of a towel. I'll show you respect.

I was ecstatic that I was able to find the zoom function on my brand new Nikon d3200. I'd caught the entire scene on tape. I'd snuck up a little closer to focus on her eyes, and when I say eyes I really mean headlights. What a nice pair she had. When I did catch a glimpse of her face, she looked pissed off. I always liked the tough ones, girls who would go toe-to-toe with any guy.

Jackson chased after her and undid her bikini top from behind. Her tits popped out.

"Holy Cow. Got Milk? Look at those beauties," I said to myself in total shock. It was my lucky day and since I'd been recording, I could look at those things any time I wanted from that point forward.

Katelyn walked over and covered her up with a towel before turning and slapping Jackson in the face. "Go easy on her. She's new to all of this."

"Sorry," said Jackson, sarcastically.

Then another young guy, clearly too young to drink ran over to Jackson and the girls, with four beers. After he passed them out he made a toast, "To a night we'll never forget," he said, as they clinked the bottles together. Damn right I wouldn't forget it. I still had the video from that day. I'd watched it nearly every day since, often pausing it on Alexa's topless, suntanned body.

CHAPTER 8

IT WAS OCTOBER 24TH, when my first interrogation began. I was just glad Katelyn bailed me out the first time around. I'd still had no clue as to why I was there or what had happened between Alexa and I. I had never done anything wrong in my entire life. Never broken a law. Never cheated on a test. Never stolen anything. Never told so much as a small fib to anyone at any time. I was just a student, a son, an employee. Nothing special. I couldn't possibly have had anything to do with this crime. *Could I?*

I was just your ordinary, American, college student. People trusted me. I helped them out with all sorts of things, their math homework, their English papers, their Science projects. So why was I the one sitting there in that cold dark room, a police woman staring back at me with a smug look on her face?

People might not have known this about me, but I was actually a hero. I'd helped drive a father's sick child to the hospital once, where the operation they performed saved her life. I'd covered at the store for another employee so that he could spend time with his girlfriend, so she wouldn't break up with him. I was not interested in overthrowing the government or assassinating the President or burning down the school. Not *me*. I was all about doing good deeds.

I was intellectual, not debonair. People should have respected me for my mind. Only they didn't. You never would see me clanking wine glasses with elegant women and bedding them that same evening. Nope. Instead assholes like Jackson Waters got to do things like that. Kissing them in their low-cut, tight-fitting dresses while chit-chatting over a plate of appetizers as they stood tall in their high-heels, gazing into his eyes.

I rode a bicycle instead of drove a car and the closest thing I'd ever had to a weapon was a small-pocket knife my father had given me for my twelfth birthday. I'd just hoped that we could get this interrogation over with quickly because I really needed to scratch my crotch.

The woman with short burgundy hair tossed a folder of photos on to the table, all of them pictures of Alexa. My first thought was one of relief. By the look on Detective Nicole Sellers's face, you would have thought I'd killed someone. "Do you know who that is Mr. Crenshaw?"

"Nope. Never seen her before in my life," I said, rather sarcastically.

"Cut the crap, Landon. We found her in bed next to you. *Naked.* Care to explain what happened last night?"

I really wished I could remember, that I could talk my way out of it but the truth was that I didn't have a fucking clue what had happened that night, other than the fact that I'd woken up next the hottie I'd been falling for since the day we met.

"I had nothing to do with this," I said, glancing at the photos of Alexa, which were giving me a massive boner under the table.

"So you're not the one who raped her?"

Her question pissed me off. "I never raped anyone!" I shouted.

"That's funny because we found you at the scene of the crime. Your semen was all over her breasts."

"I told you I didn't rape her," I shouted. "I love her. I would never hurt her."

"Is this how you show your love," said the detective, picking up the photos and shoving them in my face. "How many other girls did you show your love to this way?"

"None!"

"She was drugged you know. There were traces of Flunitrazepam in her system. "You're a smart kid, Landon. You should know what that is."

I remained silent for the time being.

"That's right Landon, it's found in Rohypnol, otherwise known as the date rape drug. You know who uses that type of drug on their victims? Rapists, like yourself," she said, jabbing her finger into my chest.

"For the last time I'm not a rapist."

"I don't believe you Landon. You just told me you loved her. There's no way a girl like her would be interested in an outcast like you."

"Stop…*please*. Just stop," I said.

"That's what happened isn't it Landon? She didn't respond to your advances, so you took it upon yourself to make it happen. To make her willing to be with you?

"I didn't do anything," I said. "I just want to go home.

"The only place you're going is a jail cell. Do you know what they do to rapists in prison? It's not pretty."

"I'm not a rapist!" I shout again.

"Landon, we've looked into your background. No criminal record, no suspensions, not even so much as an after school detention, so why do something like this? Or is this just the first time you've been caught? It says here, that you scored the highest IQ in your entire school. I'm sure someone with your intellect could easily cover up a crime. So tell me Landon, how many more are there?"

"How many what?"

"How many victims? How many other crimes did you get away with? Don't play dumb with me Landon. Start talking. We can help you, but not unless you help us. Work with me here. You've got to give me something."

"There's nothing to tell!"

"We searched your dorm room, Landon."

The detective slams a piece of paper down onto the table. "Look at that. Landon and Alexa forever. I wonder how Alexa would feel about that.

"That doesn't prove anything."

Another detective enters the interrogation room. A man this time. "Landon, I'm Detective Carson Mueller. Now my partner is trying to help you out here. So start talking and maybe we can get the DA's office to cut you a deal, but that's not going to happen if you won't tell us anything."

"I'll tell you the same thing I told her. There's nothing to tell. I didn't *do* anything. I woke up next to her and don't remember anything else. I have no idea how I got there."

"You expect us to believe that you just happened to end up in a bed next to a girl you've had a hardon for since the beginning of the semester and that *nothing* happened? That you don't remember any of it?

"I was young once too, Landon and let me tell you that if I was your age, I'd probably try to go after Alexa too. She's tall, sexy, smart, athletic. What guy wouldn't want a girl like that?

Those cops were really starting to piss me off. I just wanted to get home and catch up on some reading.

"Landon do you know what else we found at the crime scene besides your little love note? We found an interesting little video. One that has guess who? Alexa May on it. Surprise. Surprise. I'll bet you've been stalking her this whole time. What were you doing? Hiding in the bushes? How else would you get a video like that?

"I wasn't stalking."

"No? Sure looks like stalking to me. Is voyeurism your thing? I'm sure any college guy would love to see that pretty little thing topless but not all of them do. But you. You have a video of her. You could look at those things every day if you wanted to, without her consent of course."

Detective Nicole took over the room again, looking down at a file. "Look here. It says you're a forensic science major. Perfect subject for someone who wants to get away with murder."

"Wait…Who said anything about murder."

"That's what comes next, Landon. First rape, then murder."

The door barges open and Katelyn struts in looking like some sort of hooker, high-heels, low-cut top, too much makeup…and a briefcase.

"Cut him loose," she says.

"Who are you?" asked Detective Sellers.

"I'm his legal counsel. You have nothing to hold him on, so we're out of here."

"Not so fast," said Detective Carson. "This guy's not going anywhere. He raped someone."

"I've got a copy of the rape kit. There are no signs of vaginal tearing, no evidence at all that suggests my client ever penetrated the victim."

"His Semen was found splattered all over her breasts."

"Irrelevant. Could have been consensual."

"We found a video of her topless in his dorm room."

"That has nothing to do with the crime my client's been charged with. Besides I've seen the tape. Mr. Crenshaw is not on the tape and there is no proof that he's the cameraman."

"Also he was seen attending a volleyball event in which Alexa was participating and majors in forensic science."

"Detective it's not a crime to be a spectator at a sporting event, nor is it a crime to choose a major."

I had no idea why Katelyn came to my rescue but that was the day I learned what her major was. Pre-Law.

"Face it Detective. You don't have a case. "We're leaving."

CHAPTER 9

"SO…DID YOU DO IT? I wouldn't blame you if you did? She is pretty hot. I'd do her."

"What kind of question is that? You just rescued me from the cops and that's the first thing you ask?"

"I was just doing my job Landon. I really don't care if you're innocent or guilty. I'm just doing my part to get all the credits that I need."

I didn't understand her. She turned towards me. I could feel her close proximity, the intensity in her expression as she stared into my eyes.

I had this strange feeling that whatever happened the other night had something to do with the young woman sitting next to me. That same woman who I'd given a piece of Big Red gum to all those years ago.

Being in the same car with her seemed terrifying. I had to get those thoughts out of my head. She came to my rescue. She couldn't possibly have had anything to do with me getting arrested. That just wouldn't make any sense.

Katelyn took my hand into hers, intertwining her fingers with mine. Her hands were cold and soft, slightly comforting.

I could see the cab driver's eyes in the mirror, staring at us. I shot him a dirty look as Katelyn leaned in closer to me. Katelyn could see him too. "Eyes on the road," she said, scolding him.

He looked away and Katelyn draped her leg over mine. Her skirt riding up, exposing more of her sexy long legs as she wrapped her arms around my neck. "Is this why she busted me out of the big house?" I asked. "Stop it Landon. That little interrogation room was nothing compared to where you're going."

"What do you mean, where I'm going?"

"Relax, Landon, sweetie. I'm just joking with you. You're skinny ass wouldn't last a day in jail. Too bad though. I kind of have a thing for bad boys."

"I don't want to go to jail."

"Landon, I'll do whatever I can to help you stay out of jail." She then whispers in my ear, "Now how about you take me for a ride? After all, I did come to your rescue. It's the least you could do."

I had no clue why she was acting the way that she was. It just didn't make any sense. I never had any girl talk to me that way, anyone be sound so downright manipulative.

She leaned in to kiss me as her hands slipped down to my belt buckle. Her mouth was warm, the kiss soft and passionate. From the corner of my eye I could see some members if the media pointing in our direction, some chasing after our cab, but they weren't close enough to see inside. They couldn't see Katelyn in my lap, straddling me. Her kiss became more intense. Her tongue inside my mouth, pressing deeper inside as she undid my belt buckle, her other hand moving lower, inside my jeans and onto my ass.

I'd never been with anyone sexually before, never done anything more than kissed a girl. I wondered if I should have told her that I was a virgin. Yeah that's me. The virgin rapist. Think about how ridiculous that sounds.

I'd be lying if I said I wasn't enjoying her touch. When we were younger, having Katelyn in my lap would have been my dream come true but instead I was just confused. Turned on but confused. Her touch somehow seemed familiar. Both gentle and comforting. She slid my jeans down below my waist. I didn't reject her. I didn't pull away when her hands moved over my underpants. The cab came to a stop. Not sure why. We may have been stopped at a traffic light. We may have pissed off the driver. Could have been either of those things.

I felt my erection growing as she placed her hand between my legs.

She leaned in close again, nibbling my ear. "Careful Landon," she breathed. "I always get what I want."

Her words bordered on insanity. I never tried to push her away. I was curious as to what she meant by her statement. She didn't know me. We'd hardly crossed paths since elementary school. Am I being made a fool of?

I couldn't help but feel that I was doing something wrong. There I was desiring Katelyn, when my heart was with Alexa. She slid her hand up over my underpants as I slowly raised my arms above my head. I was practically naked and still trembling. Hesitant to do any of it.

Her hand caressed me, from my chest, down my thighs, and then she kissed me again. Trailing her lips down my chest to my navel. I could then feel her tongue against my thigh, and she blew gently on one certain spot, causing full on arousal.

"Condom," she mumbled from between my thighs. "There's one in my purse." I reached into her bag, still feeling her warm breath against my skin and pulled out an assortment of condoms. Some regular, some magnums, some flavored. This wasn't her first rodeo.

I could feel her looking up at me and I wondered if I should let her do the honors. I'd never used one of those things before. She pulled one of the regular sized condoms from my hand and said, "Hurry up Landon. Don't you want me?" Of course I wanted her. I would be crazy not to. Only one slight problem. She wasn't Alexa. I had wanted Alexa to be my first, and according to campus security she had been.

She climbed back up and I could feel her acrylics digging into the flesh of my shoulders, her tongue darting back into my mouth. She slid down my underpants and rolled the condom on over me. Then she slid down her knickers, slid up her skirt and I was inside of her. She was warm and moist, and I wondered if I was hurting her.

I feared that I was doing it wrong. That I would somehow fail to satisfy this woman. She looked at me and gave a sly smile at the feeling of my erection inside of her.

The cab started moving again and the sky was dim now as nightfall approached. Only the moonlight filtering in through the glass allowed me a glimpse of the beautiful features of Katelyn's body. Her breasts bouncing with every thrust. This would make a perfect photograph. Too bad those asshole cops confiscated my camera.

She spread her legs further apart, pressing her chest against mine. I was deep inside of her but still nervous. So this is what sex feels like. I've got to say it feels pretty damn good. I knew that this was all Katelyn's idea, but I still felt guilty. I looked around and noticed that it was 6:48 P.M. I noticed that Katelyn had slipped her heels off onto the floor, near the door. She used her arm and held onto the back seat to support herself, bobbing slowly above me. Her face turned to the side, her eyes shut tight. I hoped she wasn't thinking of someone other than me. Wouldn't surprise me if she was though. I wasn't much of a catch. I brushed that thought away and focused on Katelyn until I came inside of her. All of this had taken exactly four minutes. Not bad for my first time. It really happened. I'd really just had sex. Hot, naughty, consensual sex.

CHAPTER 10

I'D RETURNED TO THE DORMS and was lying awake even though it was one in the morning. I couldn't get over all the dirty looks and whispers I'd heard when I returned to campus. I thought of ways that I could make them pay. If I was going to jail, I might as well do something to earn it. People had tormented me my entire life. One time some beanpole came up to me and said, "You're like a foot shorter than me. Eww. No go." Well fuck that bitch. She better not come after me when her beloved puppy goes missing.

I gazed out the window. The sky was dark. Only illuminated by the full moon as Halloween would soon be approaching. The trees hung over the campus lawn and swung slowly, like robotic arms at the gentle breeze.

I could see a large white van down below, approaching the ravine. It stopped just before it and I could hear the rustle of leaves as two masked villains got out of the car carrying a young woman's body. I couldn't believe what I was seeing as the two masked men dumped her in the creek below. Did I really just witness murderers dumping a body? I thought about calling the cops but cops were the last thing I wanted to deal with at that point. I'd seen the body rolling down the ravine until it landed on the rocks below. Her hands restrained behind her back. The two perps looked around to make sure the coast was clear before getting back into the van and driving away. It was too dark for me to make out a license plate. I thought about going to have a look. Maybe she was still alive, and I could save her. Then I would be a hero. A hero couldn't be rapist. It could have been a chance to clear my name.

I'd heard them talking before they got into the getaway van which had a magnetic sign for a cable company stuck to the side. Cable guys my ass. "Gonna take the cops awhile to find this one," said the one on the right with a deep voice. The other had a much softer voice. "They might not find her until after snowfall. Either way no one will ever suspect their cable guys to have done something like that."

A sly, evil smile spread across one the deep-voiced one's face. "Make the call." After that they were gone as quickly as they'd come.

After the van drove away, I decided I couldn't just leave her there to rot. There was a possibility that she might even be alive. I climbed out of bed, put my shoes on and headed down to the lobby and out the revolving doors, into the courtyard. I tiptoed towards the ravine, careful not to be seen by anyone.

I should have taken pictures of what I'd seen but it all happened so fast that I didn't even think to do so. Instead I was leaving my footprints near the body like some kind of fool. I climbed down the ravine, slipping a little along the way. I could see the pale body of a young woman floating in the creek. I picked up a stick and began to poke at it. I knew I should call for help but if someone came now I would just look guilty. "Hey! Are you alright," I ask. The young woman didn't respond.

I'd never seen a dead body before. Not up close and personal. I'd never even been to an open casket funeral.

When I was twelve my older brother Daniel dared me to stay overnight in a graveyard and being the idiot that I was, I actually tried to. I lasted until midnight when our parents noticed I wasn't home yet and came to find me. That was the closest I'd ever come to being near a dead body, until I was staring one in the face, most of her body submerged in water. Only her head was above the surface. I wanted to save her, but I knew I couldn't. I thought about running away. She was already dead anyways. Nothing I could do. It was too late. My chance to be the hero had slipped away.

I'd always be nobody. A geek, a loser, a quitter. I say quitter because I had given up on nearly every dream I'd ever had. One small obstacle would hold me back and I would quit the same way I had quit the baseball team all those years ago. I got up to bat and struck out and that was the end of that. Ever since then I've struck out at life. My parents liked to call me a loser so much that I began to believe it, and my high I.Q. made me the geek of the school. I'd never be a hero, a husband, a somebody. No one would ever want me, especially after I'd been branded a rapist.

I'd never had so much drama in my life. I hung out at libraries and bookstores and kept to myself. I never pictured myself in handcuffs, being charged with the rape of the woman I love. That's right. I love you Alexa May.

Behind me I could see another young woman entering the dorms with bags of groceries. They probably weren't stocked with anything other than alcohol though. I hoped she couldn't see me in the distance. I then stubbed my toe on a rock as I tried to climb back up the ravine. That's when I heard something that sounded like a cough. I looked back and saw the young girl coughing up water. I went to try and help her and cut off her restraints. I knelt beside her with my pocket knife, trying to free her. The girl then started screaming and every light in the dorms was turned on. I started to run but I could already hear sirens.

"Down on the ground!" shouted Detective Sellers. "Drop the weapon and put your hands behind your head!

I threw my pocket knife down and did as she said. How had the cops gotten here so fast? Stupid bitch with the groceries must have tipped them off.

My entire body was shaking, other than that I was unable to move. I'd never been so panicked in my entire life. My heart was pounding, and I felt light headed as Detective Nicole slapped the cuffs onto my wrists as I heard the leaves rustle.

"You better get down here," shouted Detective Mueller from the bottom of the ravine. "Call a bus."

"Don't move Landon. You know I wanted to give you the benefit of the doubt, but it seems that every time there's a crime in the area, your fingerprints are all over it.

"We've got a body. She's barely breathing," Detective Mueller carries her up the ravine the best he can before setting her down on a pile of leaves.

An ambulance and a forensic team both arrived at the same time. The EMT's put the young woman in the ambulance and treated her, while the forensics team taped off the area and bagged the evidence. "I've got something, yelled Detective Sellers, picking up a backpack filled with one hundred thousand dollars in cash. "This yours too, Landon?" I bet when we run the tests that your fingerprints are all over this. Who'd you steal the money from?"

"Someone is setting me up. Can't you see?"

"Save it for the judge."

Then another officer read me my Miranda rights and very roughly escorted me into the back of his cop car.

I could see Detective Nicole crouching down beside the young college student who I'd never seen before in my life as the paramedics treated her. The doors shut and they drove off.

"It's not what it looks like," I said to Officer Randall Hughley. I'd noticed the name on his uniform.

"Sure it isn't," he replied, turning on his Sirens as we raced down the street.

I tried to slip out of the cuffs but it was no use. I was restrained and noticed the officer had his hand on his gun. I hoped he wasn't crazy enough to shoot me. I knew I was being paranoid but given the recent circumstances, anything seemed possible.

"So tell me Landon, what's the money for? Is it drug money? Is it your payment for putting a hit on that young woman that you left in the creek to die?"

"I already told you it's not mine? I'm sure the rubber gloves and ski mask we found in the bag weren't yours either?"

"What? No. None of those things belong to me."

"You're not a very good liar Landon. Hope you like prison, kid."

I felt sick to my stomach. I was going to throw up. Why was this happening to me? What did I do to deserve this?

CHAPTER 11

DETECTIVES MUELLER and Sellers were in the interrogation room with me as I sat in a very uncomfortable chair with my wrists cuffed. "Would you like something to drink?" asked Nicole.

"So you can get my DNA off it? I don't think so. I'm not stupid."

"Landon, the lab is going to find your DNA all over the crime scene. It's just a matter of time."

"I didn't do anything wrong."

"Landon, we have your backpack full of money, your ski mask and your semen all over the chest of the victim."

Detective Mueller places photos of college student Lynessa Parsons, her pale body in the creek, devoid of enough oxygen to survive. "You better hope she lives, for your sake. So how close were you two?"

"I've never seen that girl before in my life."

"We'd like to believe you Landon. We really would," said Detective Nicole. "Only we pulled your class schedule and it turns out you had three classes with Lynessa."

Detective Mueller continued to point at the photograph, "So, did you have a little crush on this one too, Landon. That's what happened isn't it? She rejected you and you took it upon yourself to make sure that never happened again."

"That's not what happened."

Mueller stood up and stared me down. I kept my head down as he stood beside me. "So you like to play rough?" said Mueller trying to break me. "If that girl dies, you're looking at life in prison. If you want to avoid that, I suggest you start talking."

That wasn't going to happen.

CHAPTER 12

WHEN I STEPPED ONTO CAMPUS AT EIGHT A.M. I had only two things on my mind, Alexa May, and proving my innocence. The only way to do that, was to catch the person who did it. For the first time in forever, I was full of optimism. I decided not to take my anxiety pills or any other pills I had been prescribed because I felt that I no longer needed them. They just distort my cognitive thinking ability.

Sweet temptation came over me when I saw both Katelyn and Alexa side by side in the courtyard. Katelyn lathered her body with the sweet aroma of cherry blossom body lotion before hugging Alexa and heading to class. I ran towards Alexa. I needed to clear up this whole mess.

"Alexa!" I hollered, chasing after her. The second she heard my voice, the bitch started to power walk, nearly dropping the bag full of books that was slung over her shoulder. "Alexa!" I shouted again. "Wait up!"

"I have nothing to say to you, Landon," she shouted back, looking back behind her shoulder. Damn she was cute when she was mad. I'm not sure there was anything Alexa May could do that wasn't beautiful.

I ran towards her and said, "Alexa, this is one big misunderstanding."

"Landon, you know you're not supposed to be near me. Now walk away before I call the cops."

"But…."

"Save it Landon."

Why was this happening to me? All I ever wanted to do was go to college, get an education, make lots of money and marry the princess. In this case the princess would be Alexa, the girl that currently saw me as a rapist and hated my guts.

We would make beautiful babies together and I would sit and watch as she sat reading in the evenings, twirling her hair between her fingers and smiling in my direction. Then she would seduce me, and I would lift her up and carry her into the bedroom where we would make sweet love throughout the night.

At times I thought that I was still young and had my entire life ahead of me but the stress of all those ridiculous events had started to make me feel old beyond my years. I just wanted to have a normal life, not that there's any such thing as normal.

I knew that Alexa could do much better than me. I never in my life thought of myself of handsome. I couldn't rely on my good looks or a set of six-pack abs to get girls to look my way. All I had was my mind. It's sad really, how someone can feel defeated by the age of nineteen. Where did I go wrong?

College was supposed to be a new beginning, not the beginning of the end. It was supposed to be a chance to let go of any regrets you had in the past and plan for your future. The only future I'm staring at is going to prison and becoming some guy's bitch.

Some guys are arrogant pricks, always in trouble but never get caught. Always catching the eyes of the most beautiful women. Those guys shit on people and everything seems to go their way. Nice guys like me spend their entire lives being the perfect student, the perfect son, the perfect citizen, only to be screwed over in the end.

I guess I wasn't vocal enough in life. I was always kind of shy and kept to myself. I never was the type to ask for the phone numbers of the Alexa May's of the world. Just one time I wanted to be someone's last call. The reason she came home at night.

Instead I was the guy who got his face mangled by school bullies if I didn't do their homework for them. I never got to skip class and smoke pot with the cool kids. All I got were black eyes and broken bones.

No one ever wanted to take my picture. I was never going to get a job as a male model or have my face on the cover of a magazine. Not me. I was going to make the papers alright. Only it was going to be for being a psychopath, not because I was sexy or had accomplished anything great, like finding a cure for AIDS or catching the bad guys.

I supposed I was lucky that I still had my heath. No signs of cancer or genital warts or anything like that. Can't contract STD's if no one wants to have sex with you.

Just one time I wanted to get the girl, hold her while she looked into my eyes and told me that I would be her one and only. Told me that she loved me. The type of girl that would never cheat on me or walk out on me or tell me just how fucking ugly I was.

Even if I had found a way to get out of that mess and find a woman, Alexa May would be there in the back of my mind. It was a shame that it could never be she and I but history showed that if a girl claimed you raped her, she probably wasn't going to marry you.

Most girls just saw me as some sort of malignant tumor that they desperately want to be rid of. My life to this point had been utterly terrifying. An unsupportive family, no real friends and to top it all off, rape charges.

Forensics class was about to get underway at 8:30 a.m. so I had to hurry. No chance of sitting next to Alexa though. To her, I was the scum of the Earth.

I slipped into a seat in the back of the room, where I could barely hear Professor Turner. I'm just glad she didn't ask me any questions that day. I'd been asked enough questions for one week.

When class was over, I went and sat next to a fountain filled with coins as the sun shimmered above me. I was surrounded by classmates, some of them smoking cigarettes, some of them with smoking hot bods.

"Wow!" I thought. "I'm surrounded by the future of America, and by that I meant girls with big tits."

That afternoon I found Alexa's number in the campus phone book. I rang the number to her dorm and Katelyn answered. "City morgue. You book em. we cook 'em." Always a comedian, that one. "Is Alexa there," I asked. "I'm running for student council and in need of a running mate." I was a terrible liar.

"She doesn't want to talk to you, Landon. I can't help you win your case if you don't quit with the stalkerish tendencies."

"This isn't Landon."

"I know it's you. Now go find something more productive to do other than harass Alexa."

This was really getting frustrating. The first eighteen years had been uneventful. I'd never done anything adventurous in my entire life. Never got a grade lower than an A.

When I was a kid I used to pretend that I was a movie star, fighting off bullies and rescuing the pretty girl. Kissing her in the rain and making her feel safe after a moment of weakness.

Instead I didn't even have my first date until I was sixteen and I'm not really sure going to the China Buffet even counted as a real date.

I tried to force these thoughts from my head and prepared for my next class, Biology. I could hear someone down the hall, in the chemistry lab.

I went down the dark corridor on my tiptoes, careful not to be seen. I was going to catch the culprit red handed. Possibly the same culprit who was framing me. I reached the door to the lab and touched the handle. I stopped as my heart raced a million beats per minute. I opened the door and peeked inside. I used the flashlight on my phone and shined it around the room. Nothing out of the ordinary. I calmed down and began to turn around. That's when I saw him…Jackson Waters.

CHAPTER 13

BIOLOGY REMINDED ME OF CHAMELEONS. Chameleons mean camouflage. That was the first time I'd thought about running. They couldn't arrest me if they couldn't find me. I knew that their first purpose of color change was social signaling but I always saw that as bullshit. Those things did it to hide from predators, in my case it would be to hide from the cops. I thought of buying a costume. Sporting a fake moustache, changing my hair color. *Anything.*

When class was over I put my notebook back into my backpack. The notebook that had my plans on running. I'd have to burn that notebook later, once everything was in order. I was wearing ripped up jeans from the thrift store amongst a school of rich kids.

Nothing had prepared me for college. Nothing would prepare me for jail. The dorms where small and reminded me of the military for some reason. All of the students seemed to be better looking or have more money than myself. I was simply there for one reason, to get an education.

I'd moved into the dorms mid-August, the same day as freshman orientation. I didn't think about her as I moved into the small room with the relish-colored walls. I didn't yet know her, not until that night anyways. She was gorgeous but her eyes reminded me of a woman who needed rescuing.

That day I noticed something different. The other students would stare at me and quickly avert their eyes. I was sure they had all heard my story by now. My face was plastered all over the media. It seemed that for the first time in my life I was in control. People were actually intimidated by me. It was as if they were my friends I would come to their doors and inflict terror on them.

I'd never been one to break the rules but there was something gratifying about being the intimidator for once. I felt like a badass. In reality, I wasn't much of a threat to anyone. Never again would a girl tell me I can't have her number because she lost her phone. Never again would another woman say no to Landon Crenshaw.

I was going to uncover the secret of Alexa's past and catch the bastard who had set me up. That guy was going to pay. Never again would I go through another fiasco like this one.

I was deep in thought when Katelyn sat down next to me in the courtyard, lighting up a cigarette. She leaned into me, kissing my lips. "You know Landon, my services aren't free." For Alexa I would have walked through a bed of nails but not for Katelyn.

She pressed two fingers to my lips, "Think about it," she said blowing smoke into my face, causing me to cough profusely.

Her statement was sinister. I didn't want to touch her again, although my penis thought otherwise. She wrote down her phone number and the address of a nearby hotel as she stood awkwardly before me. Her fingers gently grazing my forearm like an autumn breeze as she handed me the note.

"I trust you'll make the right decision."

I didn't want to sell my soul to the devil. I told myself that I would be making a mistake if I touched her, but I didn't have a much of a choice. I needed to clear my name and Katelyn seemed to be my only hope.

Her hand covered mine and that's when I craved the touch of a woman. I needed to feel her skin against mine. So I would have to do this. I would have to give in to the temptation that was Katelyn Jacobsen. I needed her full lips on mine, her tongue in my mouth, the caress of her hand between my thighs.

"Call me tomorrow. The offer won't be on the table forever."

CHAPTER 14

ROOM 432 AT THE HARRISON INN, was just a couple of blocks away. That's where I was to be meeting Katelyn and paying my fee for her legal services. Not that law-students were really allowed to charge you but what the hell, I wouldn't last a day in an *actual* prison.

I took some rickety old stairs up to the fourth floor and used the room key at exactly 4:48 P.M, letting myself in. Only when I got there Katelyn was nowhere to be found.

I looked for a light switch and when I finally found one I flipped it to the on position. Still no light. "Katelyn are you in here? Katelyn." No one answered. I searched the room but still no Katelyn. I ran my hands along the walls looking for some sort of clue. Nothing useful along the walls. I traced the furniture with my fingers, still nothing. I reached the dresser and could feel something sharp. It was a knife. There was a note lying next to it. I used a cigarette lighter that I carried with me for the soul purpose of being a gentleman and used the flame to make out the note. "You know what to do."

It was beginning to get creepy in there. That's when I heard a woman moaning. Not the sweet blissful moan of a woman who had just experienced multiple orgasms at the hands her great lover. No. These were the moans of a woman who needed my help.

I picked up the knife and ran towards her. I could make out a silhouette of a woman tied to a chair. It was tough to see but I could tell that her mouth was taped. I removed the tape and she started to scream.

"Shut up!" I shouted, covering her mouth with my hand. "Be quiet. I'm not going to hurt you I said, replacing the tape. I was going to use the knife to undo her restraints but the second I realized it was Alexa I couldn't risk it. She would go straight to the cops for sure.

I looked down at her, a copy of Wuthering Heights sitting on a night table next to her. What could possibly be so interesting to her about that book? She had to know I wasn't going to kill her. Why was she screaming? I would never hurt Alexa. She was my dream girl, my fantasy. My one and only.

"Are you going to be quiet?" I asked. "Be quiet and I'll remove the tape." She nodded her head. "I'm serious. Don't try anything stupid."

I couldn't believe I was acting that way right then but sometimes you had to save your own ass. That was one of those times.

"Landon, please don't hurt me."

I had been wondering if she knew it was me. Question answered.

I bent down further and took her hand into mine. She sure had small hands for such a tall girl. I hoped she wouldn't try anything. I was stronger than I looked.

"Are you okay?" I asked. "Do you want some water?"

She nodded her head with tears in her eyes. I went to the sink to get her a cup of water. She lifted her head as I poured the water into her mouth.

"Alexa I would never hurt you."

"You raped me," she said in a raspy, dry-mouthed voice. I ran to the bathroom and quickly got her some more water. "Drink. Alexa I didn't rape you. I care too much about you to hurt you like that."

"You don't care about me. All you care about is yourself."

Alexa tensed as I waved the knife in front of her. "Let me go, Landon. Please."

"Why? So you can run to the cops and tell them I raped you again. I didn't touch you and you fucking know it."

"You did rape me Landon. You drugged me and raped me. Why else would we be in the same bed?

"Alexa if you were drugged you couldn't possibly remember what happened that night. You have no idea if I or anyone at all raped you?"

"Landon, your funky spunk was all over my breasts. How do you explain that?"

I wished I had an answer for her but the truth was that I didn't. I was just as uneducated as she was about the events that occurred that night.

"Just do what I say and you won't get hurt," I said, pressing the knife to her throat.

I gently slid the knife down her arm and quickly sliced through the restraints. "Don't get up. Stay right there in that chair."

She was trembling and reached out to clutch the comforter on the nearby bed. Sunlight peeked through the gap in the curtains, creating shadows on the carpeting of the cheap motel. Alexa's heart raced as she feared for her life. She didn't know what I was going to do to her, and it terrified her. To her I would never be anything more than a rapist. I would never be her husband, her lover, her one and only.

I draped my arm over her shoulder. "Why do you think I would ever hurt you?"

"Because you raped me and now you are kidnapping me."

"I didn't do either of those things. I only came here because I was supposed to be meeting someone."

My phone rang. I let it go to voicemail.

The sunlight allowed me to see clearly and Alexa looked radiant in her green sleeveless silk top. It was a striking combination with her long brown hair. She looked into my eyes hoping to find an answer. I too needed answers. I needed them right fucking now.

I reached out my hand and my fingers glided over her spine like gentle insects. Her skin was soft, and she looked elegant in her black sequined mini. Someone had even gone through the trouble of putting her in a pair of killer high heels. That's right, someone. Not me. I had nothing to do with it. Nothing at all.

She looked nice. Not quite perfect but I could work with what was in front of me. "Would you like some tea?" I asked, noticing the hotel had some available to us. There I was in a huge predicament, asking my victim for tea. What the fuck was I thinking?

For years I was the one who felt like a prisoner and there was still a good possibility that I was going to be one but first the once time in my life I now saw someone else as the prisoner. Freedom had a price.

Her tall body leaned forward, and she crossed her arms in front of her chest, hugging her body. Never responding to my offer of a hot cup of chai.

Alexa looked both scared and adorable at the same time. I was sure she would rather be held captive by some chiseled model she'd seen at all of those book signings she'd been to. No one would want the last person they see to be me. Not that I was going to harm her. She was my everything. She just didn't know it yet. Or didn't care.

Alexa began to stand up. "Sit down!" I scolded as she tried to peek out the window. It was an usually warm day in November, and she wanted to escape, to no longer be my captive.

My cell rang again. Only once this time, reminding me of the voicemail.

I put the phone to my ear and heard Katelyn's voice. "Where are you Landon? We had plans tonight. How dare you stand me up."

I couldn't believe what I'd just heard. Stand her up? She's the one who told me to meet me at the ratty old hotel and never showed. I had to get out of there.

Quickly I tied Alexa back to the chair and ran out of the room.

Shit. I dropped the knife.

CHAPTER 15

I'D WATCHED IT COUNTLESS TIMES NOW. The video of Alexa May. It was so fucking hot. The police thought they had confiscated it but I'm not stupid. I made myself a copy before they ever had a chance to look at it. Her tits were so perky. The video also showed packs of other gorgeous college students, most in bikinis. Others staring into pocket mirrors and reapplying their makeup.

It was the first peaceful morning I'd had in weeks. I poured myself a strong cup of coffee. Added just enough cream and sugar until it looked like cardboard. That was the way it tasted best.

I took a sip and was ready to start my day. The coffee was hot just like Alexa May. My future bride. My future bride that hated my fucking guts.

I started to make myself breakfast. An omelet. Something Alexa would probably never do for me. Women of the millennium didn't seem to want to have anything to do with taking care of their men. No interest in making him a sandwich or losing weight or satisfying him sexually. I had begun to think that more men cooked than women now. Every one of them treated like a little puppy dog by their wives. Let's face it. Society had become sissified. I knew I wasn't the toughest guy, but I would never be a slave to needs of some controlling butterball of a woman.

I stopped the video when I heard a knock at the door. Two scantily clad women stood before me. Both of them looked like hookers. That's probably because they were. For the next hour Bubbles and Bambi were going to love me like I was studly.

They were right on time. They must have known just how much punctuality meant to me. The girls barged their way in to my dorm room and sat down on the couch awaiting their instructions.

I'd asked them to be discreet when I responded to their ad on Rackpage. They agreed and said they would fulfill all of my wildest fantasies. How could I possibly pass up an offer like that? It wasn't like Alexa was going to change her mind and be my girl. At least not today.

Bambi's cool blue eyes deliberately weighed upon the reaction in my jeans. I was her meal ticket. The guy who would support her shoe fetish today.

Bubbles moved her eyes towards the large protrusion in my pants as well. A down payment on her new Gucci bag. It was in that tiny dorm room that my fantasies were going to come true. I spent most of my time there. Not much to do when you are lacking friends and girls have zero interest in you unless you pay them. That day I realized just how sad and pathetic my life really was.

It was nice to have real life women showing an interest in me on this one particular day, even if they were only working girls. I watched as they started to undress. I'd become quite good at watching. You could call me Landon Crenshaw: Ultimate Voyeur. If I'd learned anything from my days behind the camera, it was that everyone had erotic aspirations and yes I do mean everyone. Your parents, your teacher, even your priest. Everyone was just looking for gratification from another person. Everyone wanted to be loved, to be touched, to be recognized. To be important to someone else.

I tried hard not to exchange glances with either of the prostitutes. If I looked them in the eyes, I would see them as people. If I saw them as people, little Landon wouldn't be up to the task.

I was stiffening as the two girls began to kiss. I'd never seen two women make out before. I decided it was something I liked very much. I had so many imaginative fantasies but somehow this one had never crossed my mind.

I wondered what the girls were thinking. If their hearts were racing the way mine was. I wondered if I seemed inexperienced to them or if I too was a fantasy of theirs. Maybe they enjoyed their profession. Getting paid to have sex. I could roll with that.

Then the two girls bent over. "Are you going to punish us Sir? Are you going to teach us a lesson?"

Bambi and Bubbles' lips smiled at me. Their eyes shone like stars.

I took a few steps towards them. "Aren't you forgetting something, Slade?"

I had told them my name was Slade to keep my discretion and because it sounded tough. Maybe even badass. Don't judge. It was my fantasy. I could be whoever I wanted.

"Forgetting something?" I questioned. "Our money dude. Pay up."

"Oh right."

I reached into my pockets and it turned out I was a little short. Short by twenty-three dollars and seventy-two cents to be exact.

"Sorry girls, this is all I have," I said handing them a crumpled up ball of cash.

"We are to be paid in full. We already showed you more than you should have seen. Don't you think we're worth it?"

"Of course you're worth it. You ladies are stunning."

"Hold him still," said Bubbles to Bambi. Bambi held my arms behind my back and sucker punched me. "Loser," she said. "That's all you'll ever be. A short, pathetic, little loser."

"I'll call the cops!" I shouted.

"No you won't," said Bubbles. We know all about you…and your rape charges. Is that what you were planning to do to us too? Rape us?"

"I'm not a rapist."

Bubbles hit me again. In the stomach that time. I was getting my ass kicked by a girl. I could picture my Dad laughing at me. The look of disappointment on his face. The same look he would give me every time I came home spitting out dirt and blood. I'd never been able to prove anything to my father. I could feel his presence standing over me. "Suck it up! I didn't raise a pussy."

While I was hunched over, Bambi released my arms and kicked me square in the nuts. I grabbed my crotch and winced in pain. These hookers had given new meaning to the term blue balls.

"What's this DVD?" asked Bubbles, pointing to the disc that had the Alexa May video."

"Nothing," I said.

"Then you won't mind if we take it," said Bambi."

"No. That's mine. Leave it."

"You shorted us. We'll take whatever we damn well please," said Bubbles.

Both ladies stared me down with disgruntled looks on their faces. "Have a great day Landon. Loser. Tell Katelyn we said hello."

CHAPTER 16

I GOT ON MY BICYCLE and set out to find new material for the spank bank. I didn't bother to put anything on my black eye. No ice. No meat. No frozen peas. How's that for tough? Huh Pop? The bike seat was hell on the Chiclets though. One seemed to be okay but the other might have needed a body cast and set of crutches. The things I go through for you Alexa May.

I knew the cops would come looking for me once they found Alexa. Until then I had planned to stay under the radar. That's why I picked up a new ball cap and some dark clothes. I rode to the other end of the campus, near the school library. I knew that Alexa would be there studying.

I chained up my bike and took the elevator up to the fourteenth floor. That's where I found her. My dream girl had her nose buried in a book as usual. She looked fine to me. Nothing about her, indicated that she was a rape victim. I was a bit surprised that she was still attending classes with all the things she had claimed to be going though. For all I knew she was setting me up. I didn't rape her. I sure as hell didn't kidnap her. She could have planned the entire thing herself. She was highly intelligent. I quickly erased those thoughts from my head. My Alexa would never do that to me.

She was so beautiful, elegant. Like a tall, clear glass of water filled with love. Love of life, love for me. Well, maybe someday.

Throughout my entire life, Alexa was the only girl I had ever met that I envisioned a future with. Until the night in the hotel room, I had been embarrassed to tell her just how I felt about her. I wanted to walk over to her and tell her again just how much I loved her and her olive skin. I wanted to tell her that I loved when she let her hair down and how it draped perfectly over her shoulder. I wanted to tell her that she looked so cute when she chewed her food. I wanted to tell her that I wanted to marry her.

Only that couldn't happen. To her I was just a creepy rapist, stalker. To her I was a bad guy. Girls love bad boys. They don't love bad guys. They want a man who makes their heart flutter, not one who makes it stop.

I stood behind the bookshelves with sore nuts and a black eye, peeking through the stacks. I never should have bought those hookers. But why did they mention Katelyn? It seemed that every time something bad happened to me of late, Katelyn appeared or was mentioned. Was it possible that I was being framed by my own lawyer?

I crouched down and pressed record on my camera. I watched as she gazed out the window, twisting the spirals of her wet hair into a ponytail.

She was wearing too many clothes that day. I liked my other video so much better. Still, she had a face as bright as the sun, tan and wavering. I loved her features, even if they say the camera adds fifteen pounds. They had been stuck in my mind from the moment I'd met her. There was no one as extravagantly beautiful as Alexa May.

Her heart-shaped necklace shifted with the turn of the page. My camera angle giving me a slight glimpse of her cleavage. I didn't recall her wearing a necklace before and I wondered if that particular pendant had any sort of meaning behind it. If it was given to her by her father. A dead grandparent. An ex-boyfriend perhaps. I needed to know more. I couldn't get enough of Alexa May. I needed to know every intimate detail of her life.

I needed to know what she used to make her hair smell so good. What body lotion she preferred. How she drank her coffee. If she preferred Mozart or Chopin. Most of all I needed to know if she would ever date a geeky guy like myself. If she could ever fall in love with me.

I could still see the hurt that lurked in her eyes. Pain that she believed I'd caused her. There also seemed to be darkness in them, something that hadn't been there before. They looked almost animalistic.

She stirred in her chair as a gleam of light shone through the window. Every time I looked her way it was like staring at a piece of fine art.

I knew I had to be more careful what I did and what I said if I was going to stand a chance with Alexa May, the little white liar. Telling everyone I raped her. As much as I cared for her, she didn't know whether or not she was raped at all. She needed to close that mouth and hush up that turpentine tongue before someone really got hurt. I'm not a bad man but when you push people to the edge, it makes them do crazy things. Things they wouldn't normally do. Things they would no longer regret.

I wasn't someone you would have called "lucky." Though if I really did get to hook up with Alexa, one might call me that.

I had to stop being a pessimist. I had to believe in my mind that everything would work out for the best. I wanted a fresh start. To move to a new state. Go to a new school. Only moving away would mean, no more Alexa May, and I just couldn't handle that.

I needed what you would call a man's makeover. A new hair style, more muscles, new clothes and a tattoo that told a story written upon my chest. I needed to be the perfect man. The perfect man with perfect flaws. That's what really attracted women. Not the slutty Katelyn's of the world but real women. Women with class. Women who wouldn't cheat. Women who made you feel like you were the most important guy in the world. Women who would support you until the end. Women like Alexa May. Someday Alexa would be mine. I just had to keep the new found confidence I'd woken up with that morning. Then she wouldn't see me as a kidnapping, stalking rapist. She would see me as a man. Her man.

The world had pissed me off for the last time. No more moping. No more sitting on the couch playing video games. It was time to take action. Time to fix, no, fine tune everything that was broken in my life.

There were so many differences between Alexa and I. She was water and I was oil. She was wanted by men. I was wanted by the cops. It seemed that in the college world it didn't matter how you felt about someone because in college looks meant everything. So I decided to bite my lip and man up. If women wanted men who looked good, then that's exactly what I was going to make happen for myself. I would eat right, replacing McDonald's with a veggie tray and hit the gym as often as I could. I had never wanted to conform to society but if I started to look like the model citizen that women desired, maybe, just maybe I'd get out of this mess somehow. Nothing wrong with wanting to improve my life.

For as long as I could remember, everyone hated me. My father hated me. The other students hated me. Hell, even I hated me.

Only things were going to be different for me from now on. I was going to get out of this rut, finish college and buy a big house with a pool. A pool that beautiful women in thong bikinis would stop over to swim in or sit poolside while I rubbed tanning oil all over their perfect bodies.

Then someday Alexa would come to my door and see how far I'd gotten in life. She'd have no choice but to want to be with me, seeing my chiseled body and the security I could provide for her. At that point I would ask all of the other ladies to leave, lift Alexa into my big strong arms and give her a deep passionate kiss. Welcome home Alexa May.

That's when it happened. When I saw all of those S.W.A.T. team members coming towards me. Let them arrest me if they want. Women love bad boys.

"Down on the ground. Landon Crenshaw you're under arrest for the kidnapping and rape of one Miss Alexa May." I put my hands behind my head, dropping my camera to the floor as I fell to my knees. I should have been angry and pissed off and wanted to kill them for blaming me for such a ridiculous crime but instead I kept my mouth shut.

Some fat cop led me down the narrow rows of the library with the barrel of his gun pressed against my hip. All of the other students were staring at me. I just smiled. I would have waved too if my hands weren't restrained. Fuck 'em. I'm Landon Crenshaw. I'm a badass.

Every step towards the county jail should have felt like

hell on me. Instead I rather enjoyed the felon's walk of shame. I didn't care if people stared. It was hard to believe that this was happening to me but I no longer looked at that moment as the end. It was a whole new beginning. If I got out of that somehow, no longer would I settle for good, not great. Playtime was over. It was time to buckle down and be the man my father had always wanted me to be.

When we got to the county jail after a twenty minute ride in the back of a cop car, I was led down another long corridor, passing cell after cell. Each cell looked identical, with the exception of the writing on the walls. Some done in graffiti, some in foreign languages I couldn't quite make out.

Most of the men were huge, tattooed and every one of them looked like they'd killed someone and enjoyed it. "Hey sexy, you got a cigarette!" shouted the only thin man, one wearing makeup. "Damn you are one fine piece of ass." That was the first time I'd been hit on by a man. No I did not enjoy it. I know that I should have been scared but convicts can smell fear the same way dogs can. Show fear and they'll tear you apart. I did my best to look tough. To look like the badass rapist that everyone thought I was.

At the end of the corridor, the officer nudged his gun into me and pushed me into what would be my cell.

So this is where it all begins.

CHAPTER 17

THEY'D GIVEN ME THE RIGHT TO A SPEEDY TRIAL. Less than a month after my capture, I was about to stand trial for crimes I didn't commit. The verdict was to be handed down that day, November 12th. I looked spiffy in my new suit. Got myself a new haircut and though I hadn't yet accepted, one of the inmates offered to give me a free tattoo. I was ready to get this thing over with and get on with my life.

Alexa May looked delicious in her sequined shirt and black skirt. She looked like the girl who would someday cook me dinner and bring me a beer. She looked like my kind of girl.

Right now she only saw me as a vicious rapist. The guy who drugged her and made her take it rough like a whore.

That's when I began to think seriously about all the events that had occurred and how meeting Alexa had turned my entire life upside down. So why did I still love her?

As I was deep in thought, Katelyn walked in wearing one of those hideous pant suits, ready to defend my honor. You know what I'm talking about, those things that no woman should be allowed to wear. They are equivalent to skinny jeans on a man. Now that's a real crime.

Alexa's lawyer entered the courtroom just after Katelyn. He looked old, experienced. The type of old school guy who would seek the ultimate penalty for someone who had harmed someone of the female sex. That was the last thing I needed.

He was very well-known. A smart, courageous lawyer named Bob Corvine. He'd only lost one case in twenty years. It was his first and only loss. Not one time since, did he come close to losing in court. I was probably going to jail but at least I'd be famous for something. Maybe one day I'd be able to tell my story to the world and possibly even get a book deal out of it.

Judge Anelia Nelson sat down at the bench in her black robes, looking as if she wanted me to rot in hell. Not a good sign for me. All the evidence was stacked against me. The semen on the victim. My fingerprints on the knife. Even the mention of me videotaping Alexa May. Things seemed hopeless for me. For the old me, anyways. The new me was ready to take on the world. Que the *Rocky,* soundtrack, kick ass and take names.

"Let him hang until he's dead!"

"Have a guy with AIDS bareback him!"

"I'll kill him for you!"

Judge Nelson slammed down her gavel. "There will be order in my courtroom, slamming it down so hard she nearly put a dent in her bench.

Still they wouldn't shut up. The people in Lyndall, Ohio had no respect for rapists, kidnappers either. Those disgruntled citizens wanted me dead.

"Another word and you will be escorted out," shouted Judge Nelson.

I had once thought this would be an easy victory for me, considering my only crime was loving the wrong woman.

Judge Nelson glared over her glasses at me, intimidating everyone in the room.

"I hope he rots in hell. I hope he gets ass fucked by a porcupine!" shouted Alexa.

Harsh words, coming from my future queen.

"Mr. Corvine, calm your client down."

"Yes your honor," he said, whispering in Alexa's ear.

Katelyn rubbed my thigh. "It's going to be okay Landon. I'm good at what I do. They don't have enough to convict you."

This coming from a girl who was hooked on Mary Jane. Very reassuring.

There had been a two hour recess before we'd gotten to that point and I needed a drink. Something strong. Something that would take the pain away. Something that would take me away from the horrid reality that was about to be my life. A life spent in behind bars.

I'd lost my appetite and hadn't had any lunch. I wasn't sure how anyone could be hungry when facing the type of predicament I was in. The news was outside. People had cancelled their meetings to watch this trial. They wanted nothing more than to see me pay for my crimes. Only they weren't my crimes. Someday the real culprit would be caught, and everyone would see just how idiotic our judicial system was. Then I would sue them for as much as I could.

I was sweating. It must have been one hundred and five degrees in that courtroom that day. There were fans going, but they just seemed to be blowing more hot air.

Looking over to the jury the judge said, "Have we reached a verdict?"

"We have your honor."

I took a deep breath. Soon, my life would change forever.

To me it was an easy choice for the jury. While some things looked bad for me, there really wasn't any proof that I'd ever done anything to harm Alexa May.

They hadn't even announced whether or not I was guilty, and I was ready to jump up and down and shout objection. I was squirming in my seat like a woman who'd just gotten her period and looked over towards the jury. Each one of them had fury in their eyes. There was no way I was getting out of those charges. Good thing I'd already had my escape plan ready. That's the one positive to being a genius. No matter how bad things get, you can always find a way out.

"Please rise," said, Judge Nelson, pointing her finger in my direction.

So that was it. They might have well been reading me my last rights.

I stood up from my chair, Katelyn standing beside me.

"Remember what I told you Landon. Only the truth can set you free. It's in the Bible."

I had to chuckle at the fact that someone like Katelyn had ever read a Bible verse. "Landon, if you told them the truth, you'll be fine. You told them the truth on the stand right?"

"Yes."

"Then you've got nothing to worry about."

Again the judge motioned towards the jury. "On the count of rape in the second degree, how do you find?"

"We find the defendant, Landon Crenshaw....."

~ To Be Continued...~
ABOUT THE AUTHOR

About the Author

NJ Salupo is the author of Erotic Romance, Physiological Thrillers, and Mystery Suspense novels. Residing In Ohio he's written the majority of his life. Happy to be living the dream of being an author, NJ hopes to never wake from it. He loves his fangirls and readers, knowing his journey wouldn't be possible without their support. He is available for signing and takeovers through Facebook here: https://www.facebook.com/N.J.Salupo

www.ingramcontent.com/pod-product-compliance
Lightning Source LLC
Chambersburg PA
CBHW030824060726
47590CB00004B/1380